Clocks and More Clocks

by Pat Hutchins

Aladdin Paperbacks

Aladdin Paperbacks
An imprint of Simon & Schuster
Children's Publishing Division
1230 Avenue of the Americas
New York, NY 10020
First Aladdin Paperbacks edition 1994
Also available in a hardcover edition from
Simon & Schuster Books for Young Readers
Printed in Hong Kong
10   9

Library of Congress Cataloging-in-Publication Data
Hutchins, Pat, date.
Clocks and more clocks / by Pat Hutchins.—1st Aladdin Books ed.
p.   cm.
Summary: Not one of Mr. Higgins's four clocks kept the same time until the Clockmaker
assured him they were all correct.
ISBN 0-689-71769-5
[1. Clocks and watches—Fiction.]   I. Title.
PZ7.H96165C1   1994
[Fic]—dc20   93-11208

For Lily Goundry

One day Mr. Higgins found a clock in the attic.

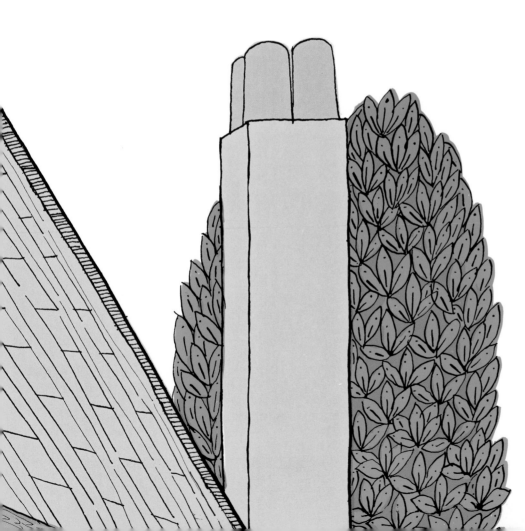

It looked very splendid
standing there.

"How do I know if it's correct?" he thought.

So he went out
and bought another

which he placed
in the bedroom.

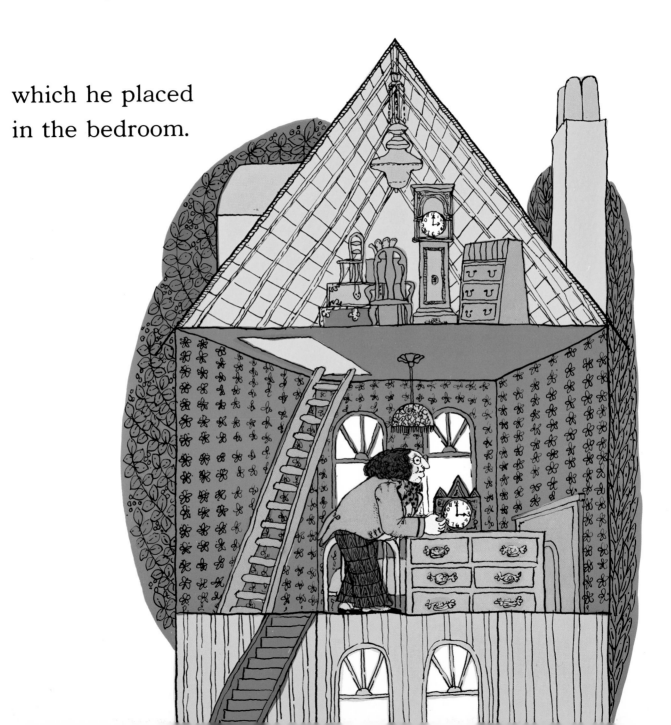

"Three o'clock," said Mr. Higgins.
"I'll see if the other clock is right."

He ran up to the attic,
but the clock said
one minute past three.
"How do I know which one
is right?" he thought.

So he went out and bought another

which he placed
in the kitchen.
"Ten minutes to four,
I'll check the others."

He ran up to the attic. The attic clock said eight minutes to four.

He ran down to the bedroom.
The bedroom clock said
seven minutes to four.
"I still don't know which one
is right," he thought.

So he went out
and bought another

which he placed
in the hall.
"Twenty minutes
past four," he said,

and ran up to the attic.
The attic clock said
twenty-three minutes past four.

He ran down to the kitchen. The kitchen clock said twenty-five minutes past four.

He ran up to the bedroom. The bedroom clock
said twenty-six minutes past four.
"This is no good at all," thought Mr. Higgins.

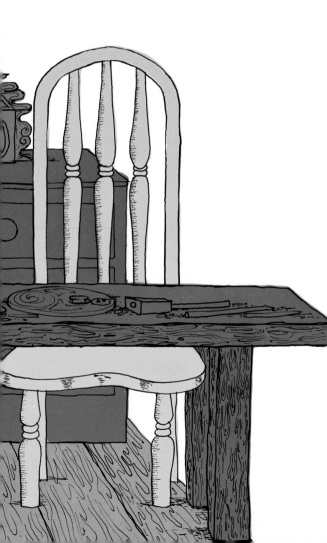

And he went to the Clockmaker.
"My hall clock says
twenty minutes past four,
my attic clock says
twenty-three minutes past four,
my kitchen clock says
twenty-five minutes past four,
my bedroom clock says
twenty-six minutes past four,
and I don't know which one
is right!" said Mr. Higgins.

So the Clockmaker
went to the house
to look at the clocks.

The hall clock said five o'clock.
"There's nothing wrong with this clock,"
said the Clockmaker. "Look!"

The kitchen clock said one minute past five.
"There!" shouted Mr. Higgins.
"Your watch said five o'clock."
"But it is one minute past now!"
said the Clockmaker. "Look!"

The bedroom clock said two minutes past five.
"Absolutely correct!" said the Clockmaker.
"Look!"

The attic clock said three minutes past five.
"There's nothing wrong with this clock either,"
said the Clockmaker. "Look!"

"What a wonderful watch!" said Mr. Higgins.

And he went out
and bought one.
And since he
bought his watch

all his clocks
have been right.